Black Spot

거울을 봤는데 얼굴에 검은 반점이 나 있어.
언제부터 있었던 거지?

I saw a black spot on my face in the mirror.
How long has it been there?

오늘? 아니, 아주 오래전. 어쩌면 태어날 때부터.

Today? No, a long time ago.
It might have been there since I was born.

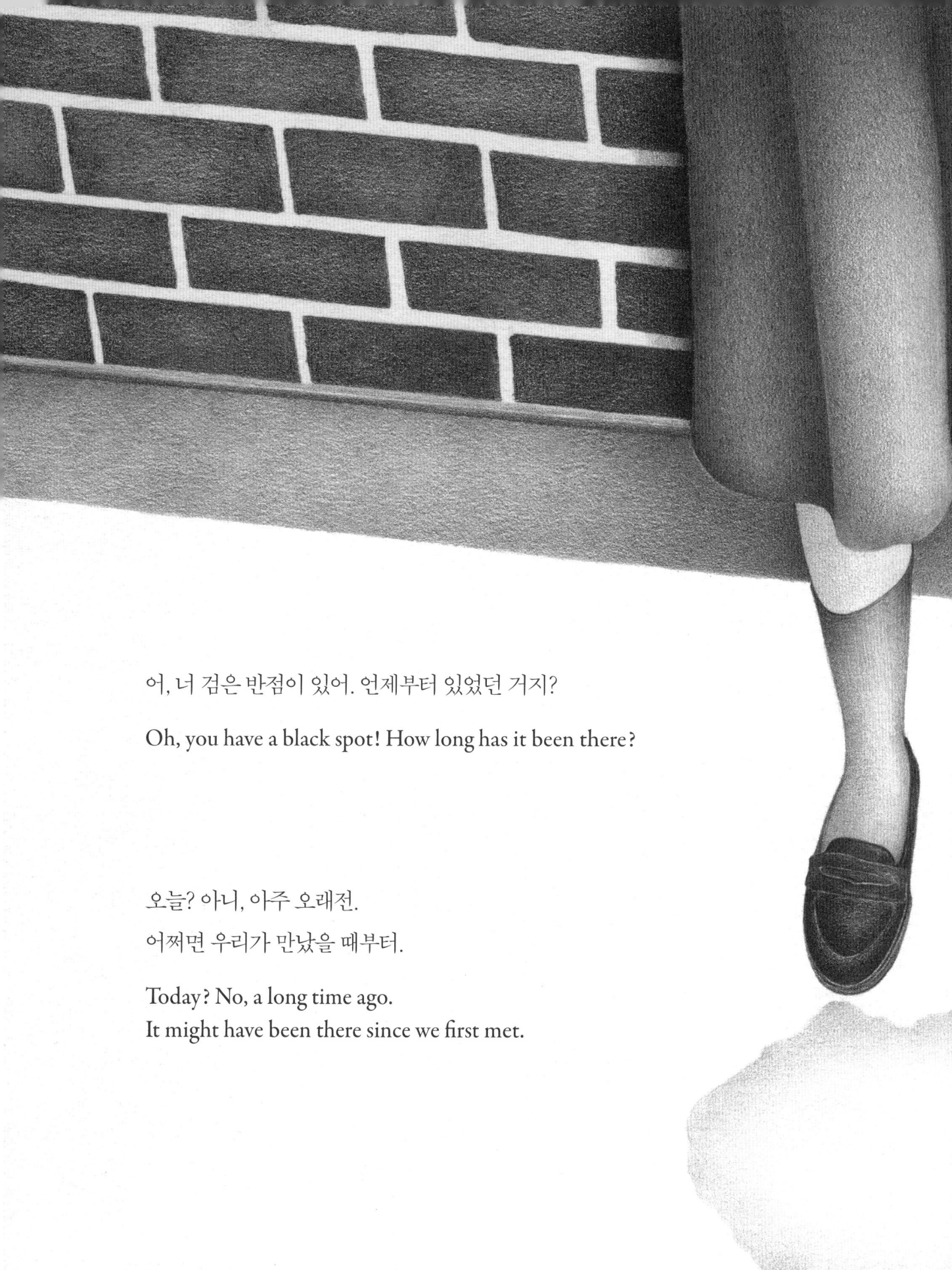

어, 너 검은 반점이 있어. 언제부터 있었던 거지?

Oh, you have a black spot! How long has it been there?

오늘? 아니, 아주 오래전.
어쩌면 우리가 만났을 때부터.

Today? No, a long time ago.
It might have been there since we first met.

사람들이 내 검은 반점만 쳐다보는 것 같아.
손으로 가려도 보고 마스크를 써 보기도 했어.

Many people might look at my black spot.
I used to hide the spot with my hands and mask it.

그럴수록 반점은 점점 커지는 거야.

No matter how hard I tried to get rid of it, it always gets bigger and bigger.

엄마와 목욕탕에 갔어.
깨끗이 씻으면 반점이 사라지지 않을까.

I went to a public bathhouse with my mother.
I had an idea that if I cleaned my body, the spot might disappear.

아무리 씻어도 지워지지 않아.

아프기만 할 뿐.

No matter how I scrubbed, it would not rub out.
Instead, it was very painful.

엄마 등에 나와 똑같이 생긴 반점이 있어.
언제부터 있었지?

I found the same spot that I have on my mother's back.
How long has it been there?

오늘? 아니, 아주 오래전. 어쩌면 엄마가 태어날 때부터.

Today? No, a long time ago.
It might have been there since she was born.

얼마나 검냐고?

How black is the spot?

반들반들 잘 깎인
검은 자갈만큼.
나무가 타고 남은
검은 재만큼.
별이 물러간 우주의
검은 구석만큼.

As black as glossy
cobblestones that are
well cut down.
As black as black ashes
after they have burned out.
As black as the universe after
all the stars have dimmed.

나와 똑 닮은 반점을 가진 사람을 만났어.
언제부터 있었던 거야?

I met a person who has the same spot as I have.
How long has it been there?

오늘? 아니, 아주 오래전. 네가 태어날 때부터.

Today? No, a long time ago.
It might even have been there when you were born.

네 반점을 보고 있으면 마음이 고요해져.

I feel calm, looking at your spot.

내 반점보다 네 반점이 더 예뻐서 그런 걸까.
더 커서 그런 걸까.
더 검어서 그런 걸까.
아니. 우리의 반점은 똑 닮았어.

Is your spot more beautiful than mine?
Is yours larger than mine?
Is yours blacker than mine?
Oh, no. Our spots are quite alike.

얼마나 닮았어?
쌍둥이의 눈, 코, 입처럼.
잘 들어맞는 양 문짝처럼.
반으로 딱 접히는 팬케이크처럼.

How similar are they?
As similar as twin's eyes, noses, and mouths.
As similar as nicely fit double doors.
As similar as a pancake perfectly folded in half.

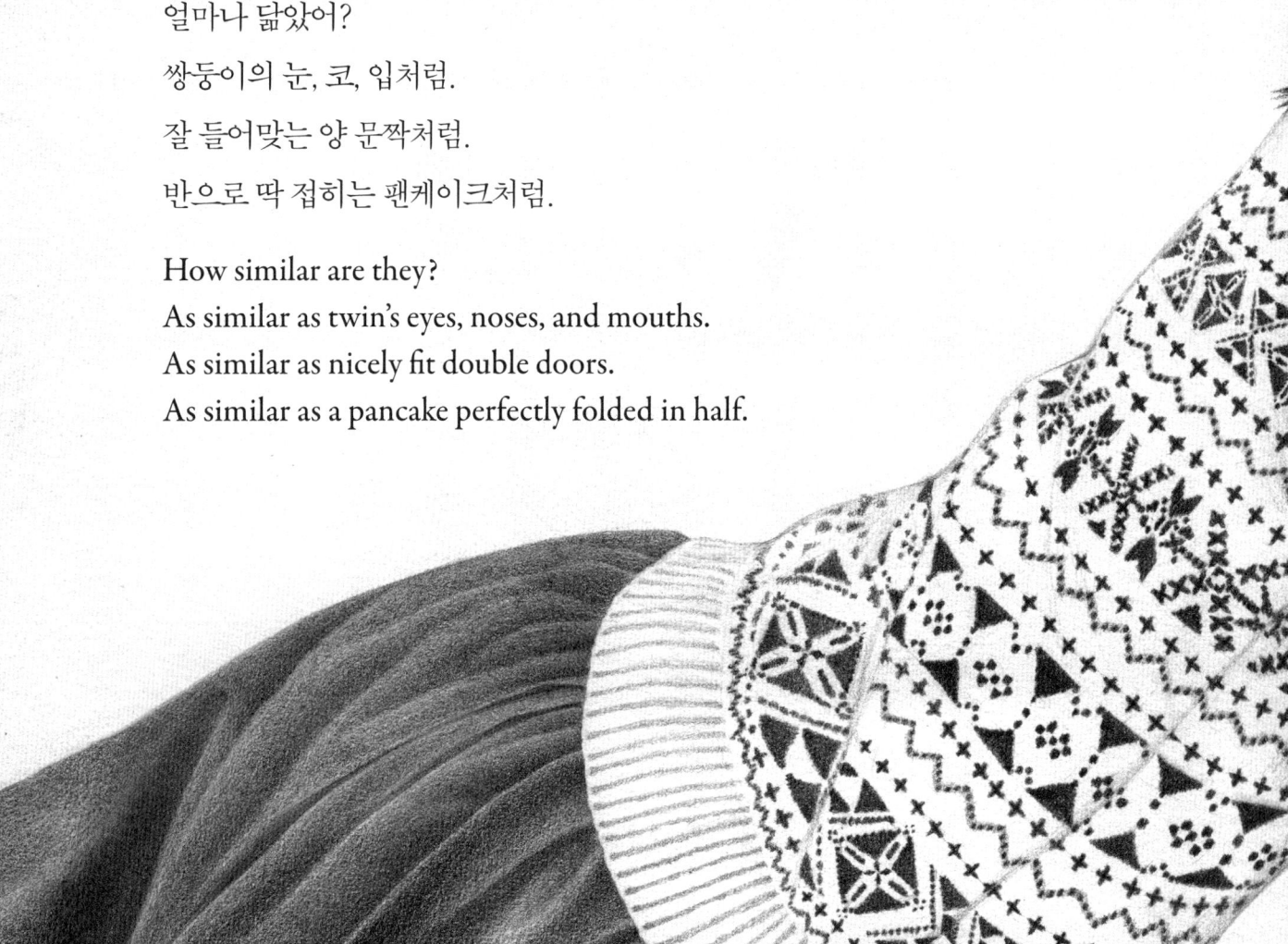

이상한 일이지?
점점 나와 닮은 네 반점이 보기 싫어져.

Is there something wrong with me?
I have gradually come to dislike your spot that is so similar to mine.

네 잘못은 아니야.
그냥 네 반점이 싫을 뿐이야.
아니야. 그냥 내 반점이 싫을 뿐이야.

It's not your fault.
I just don't like your spot.
No, actually I dislike my spot.

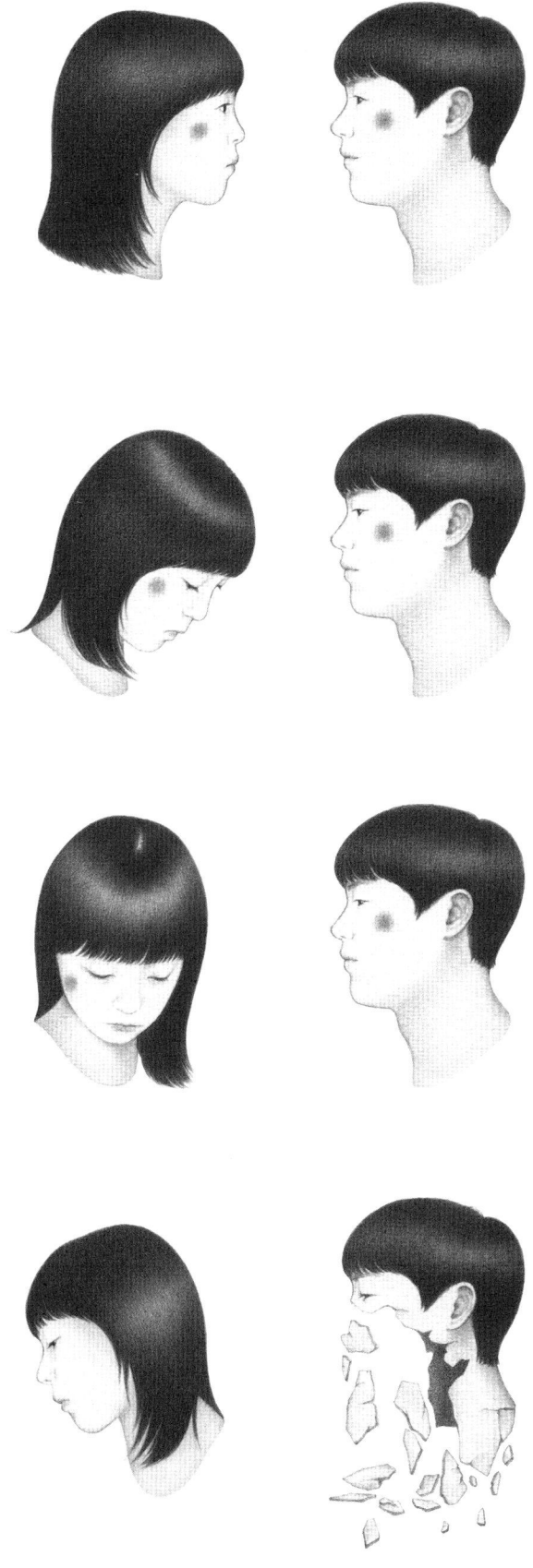

모두 검은 반점 때문이야.

This is all caused by the black spot.

내 몸에 검은 반점이 난 걸까.

Does the black spot come from my body?

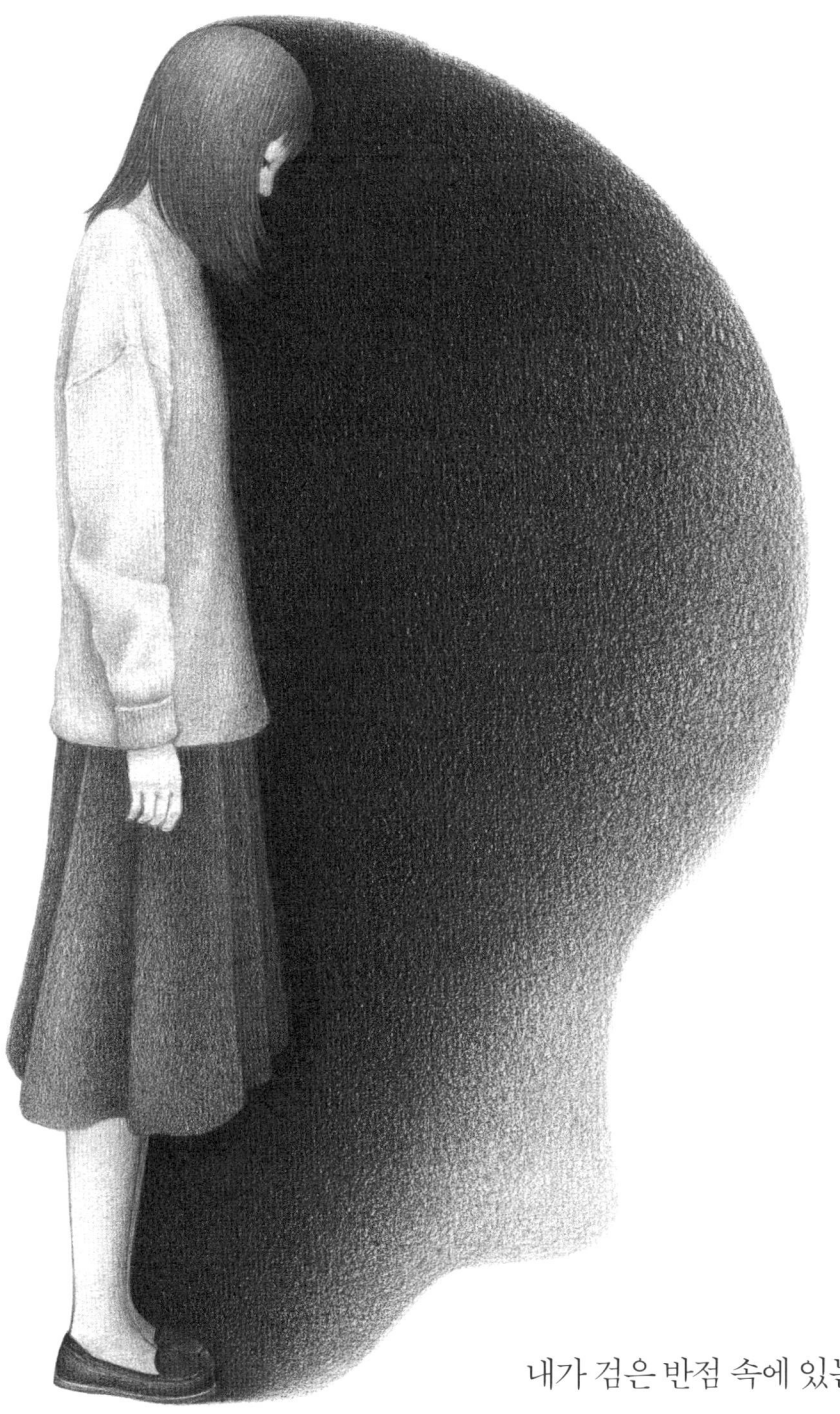

내가 검은 반점 속에 있는 걸까.

Does my body come from the black spot?

사람들이 다 내 반점만 보고 있는것 같아.

People might only look at my black spot.

모두 검은 반점 때문이야.
모두 검은 반점 때문이야.

This is caused by the black spot.
This is caused by the black spot.

어느 날 옆 사람의 몸에서 주황색 반점을 발견했어.

One day, I find an orange spot on my neighbor's knee.

저 사람 이마에 보라색 반점

A violet spot on a man's forehead.

저 여자 팔꿈치에 초록색 반점

A green spot on a woman's elbow.

저 할아버지 발목에 갈색 반점

A brown spot on an old man's ankle.

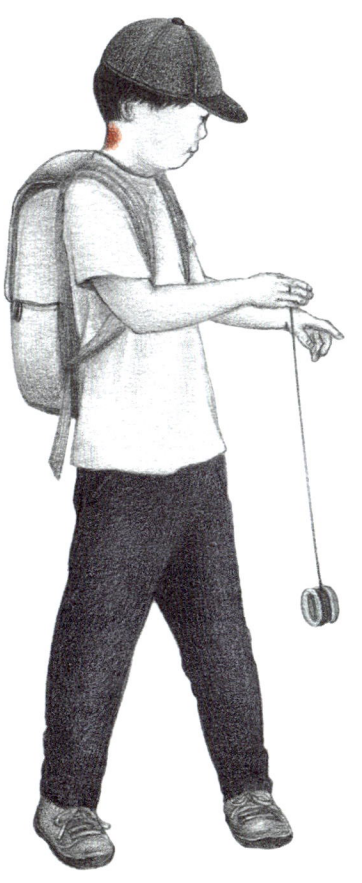

저 소년의 목에 빨간색 반점

A red spot on a boy's neck.

세상엔 온갖 색깔의 반점들이 퍼져 있어.
언제부터 그랬지?

Many different colors of spots are all over the world.
How long has this been?

오늘? 아니, 아주 오래전. 우주가 생겨날 때부터.

Today? No, maybe it was a long time ago.
They may have been there when the universe was created.

우리 속에 반점이 있는 걸까.
반점 속에 우리가 있는 걸까.

Are the spots in us?
Are we in the spots?

잘못 본 걸까?

세상이 반점들 때문에 빛나는 것 같아.

Am I looking at this all wrong?
Maybe the world glitters because of the spots.

얼마나 멋지냐고?

How beautiful is the world?

모두 🌈 반점 때문이야.

All that is caused by a 🌈 spot.

거울을 보니 얼굴에 검은 반점이 _____ .
언제부터일까?

The black spot looks _____ on my face in the mirror.
How long has it been there?

오늘? 아니, 아주 오래전. 내가 태어났을 때부터.

Today? No, it was a long time ago.
It has been there since I was born.

-

정미진
이야기를 만들고 책으로 엮어 내는 일이 즐겁습니다.
글을 쓴 책으로 〈있잖아, 누구씨〉〈깎은 손톱〉〈잘자, 코코〉
〈뼈〉〈휴게소〉〈해치지 않아〉등이 있습니다.

황미옥
물음표를 그리듯 그림 그리고 있습니다.
고양이 만지의 온갖 방해를 이겨내고 그린 〈검은 반점〉이
내게 첫 번째 답이 되었습니다.

at|noon *books*

정오의 따사로움과 열정을 담은
어른들을 위한 그림책을 만듭니다.

검은 반점

초판3쇄 발행일 2019년 9월 5일
초판4쇄 발행일 2023년 6월 2일

글   정미진
그림   황미옥
번역   방종수
펴낸곳   atnoon books
펴낸이   정미진
디자인   권으뜸
교정   엄재은
등록   2013년 08월 27일 제 2013-000257호
주소   서울시 마포구 연남로 30

홈페이지 www.atnoonbooks.net
인스타그램 atnoonbooks
유튜브 atnoonbooks
연락처 atnoonbooks@naver.com

ISBN 979-11-952161-7-8
이 책의 글과 그림의 일부 또는 전부를 재사용하려면
반드시 저작권자의 동의를 얻어야 합니다.
ⓒ 정미진, 황미옥 2016

이 도서의 국립중앙도서관 출판시도서목록(CIP)은
서지정보유통지원시스템 홈페이지(http://seoji.nl.go.kr)와
국가자료공동목록시스템(http://www.nl.go.kr/kolisnet)에서
이용하실 수 있습니다.(CIP제어번호: CIP2016026998)

정가 16000원

이 책은 마포 디자인·출판 진흥지구 협의회(DPPA)의
출판지원사업의 도움을 받았습니다.